THE VILLAGE BLACKSMITH

"The Village Blacksmith" by Henry Wadsworth Longfellow from *The Knickerbocker or New York Monthly Magazine* vol. XVI. New York; 1840. Illustrations copyright © 2020 by G. Brian Karas. All rights reserved. No part of this book may be reproduced, transmitted, or stored in an information retrieval system in any form or by any means, graphic, electronic, or mechanical, including photocopying, taping, and recording, without prior written permission from the publisher. First edition 2020. Library of Congress Catalog Card Number pending. ISBN 978-1-5362-0443-8. This book was typeset in Alike Angular. The illustrations were done in mixed media. Candlewick Press, 99 Dover Street, Somerville, Massachusetts 02144. visit us at www.candlewick.com. Printed in Shenzhen, Guangdong, China. 20 21 22 23 24 25 CCP 10 9 8 7 6 5 4 3 2 1

THE VILLAGE BLACKSMITH

Henry Wadsworth Longfellow

illustrated by G. Brian Karas

CANDLEWICK PRESS

Thank you to my son Bennett for his help
with all things Blacksmith.

Thank you to Marsha Trattner of She-Weld for showing
new blacksmiths the way and keeping this art form alive.

And thank you to Brenda Bowen for sparking
the idea of this book.

G. B. K.

U
nder a spreading chestnut tree
The village smithy stands;

The smith, a mighty man is he,
With large and sinewy hands;
And the muscles of his brawny arms
Are strong as iron bands.

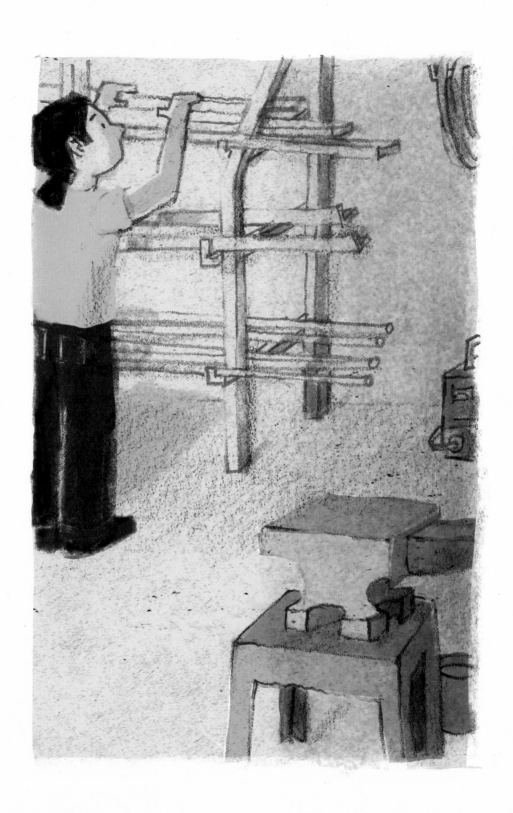

His hair is crisp, and black, and long;
His face is like the tan;
His brow is wet with honest sweat;

He earns whate'er he can,
And looks the whole world in the face,
For he owes not any man.

Week out, week in, from morn till night,

You can hear his bellows blow;

You can hear him swing his heavy sledge,

With measured beat and slow,

Like a sexton ringing the old kirk chimes
When the evening sun is low.

And children coming home from school
Look in at the open door;

They love to see the flaming forge,
And hear the bellows roar,
And catch the burning sparks that fly
Like chaff from a threshing-floor.

He goes on Sunday to the church,
And sits among his boys;

He hears the parson pray and preach,
He hears his daughter's voice,
Singing in the village choir,
And it makes his heart rejoice.

It sounds to him like her mother's voice,
Singing in Paradise!
He needs must think of her once more,
How in the grave she lies;
And with his hard rough hand he wipes
A tear from out his eyes.

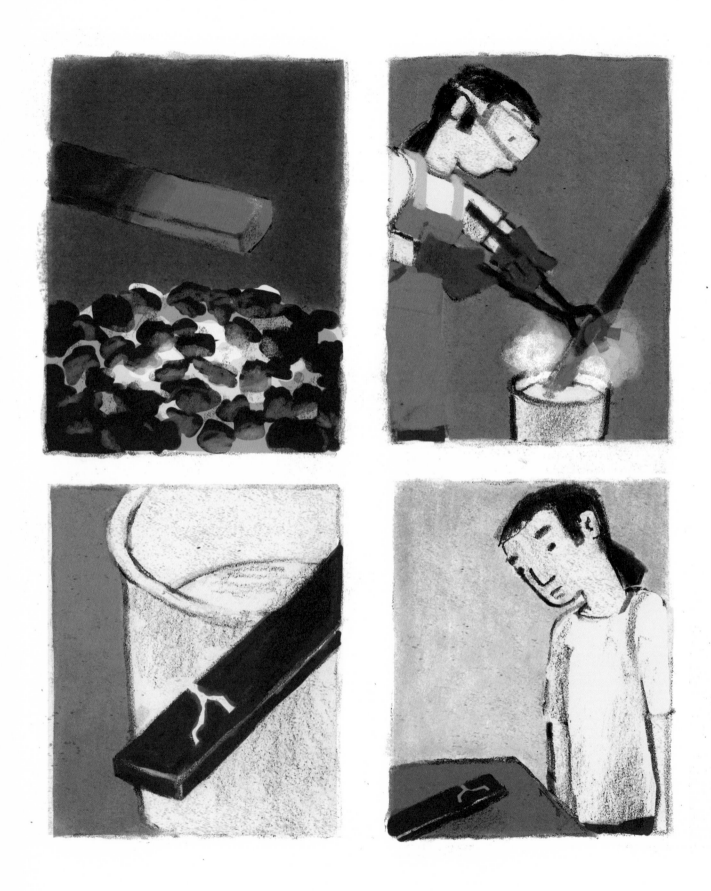

Toiling — rejoicing — sorrowing —
Onward through life he goes:

Each morning sees some task begin,
Each evening sees it close;

Something attempted — something done,
Has earned a night's repose.

Thanks, thanks to thee, my worthy friend,
For the lesson thou hast taught!
Thus at the flaming forge of Life,
Our fortunes must be wrought,
Thus on its sounding anvil shaped
Each burning deed and thought.

A BLACKSMITH'S
Tools of the Trade

TONGS

BELLOWS

A FORGE

HAMMERS

AN ANVIL

Water for
QUENCHING

Blacksmiths heat metal in coal- or gas-fired FORGES. They use BELLOWS to fan the flames and TONGS for handling the hot metal. HAMMERS pound the softened, heated metal into shape on the ANVIL.

The metal cools quickly and must be reheated in the forge if more shaping needs to be done. The pounded metal is then put in water or oil for QUENCHING. This tempering not only cools the metal but also strengthens it and gives it flexibility.

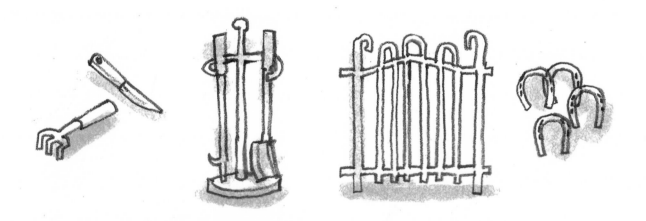

Blacksmiths have been part of society since around 1500 BCE. With their ability to shape metal, they can make tools for the garden, fireplace, or kitchen. They can also make horseshoes, gates, fences, and other decorative ironwork.

My son is a blacksmith. Many of the tools you see in this book can be found in his workshop. — G. B. K.

The Village Blacksmith

HENRY WADSWORTH LONGFELLOW

Under a spreading chestnut tree
The village smithy stands;
The smith, a mighty man is he,
With large and sinewy hands;
And the muscles of his brawny arms
Are strong as iron bands.

His hair is crisp, and black, and long;
His face is like the tan;
His brow is wet with honest sweat;
He earns whate'er he can,
And looks the whole world in the face,
For he owes not any man.

Week out, week in, from morn till night,
You can hear his bellows blow;
You can hear him swing his heavy sledge,
With measured beat and slow,
Like a sexton ringing the old kirk chimes
When the evening sun is low.

And children coming home from school
Look in at the open door;
They love to see the flaming forge,
And hear the bellows roar,
And catch the burning sparks that fly
Like chaff from a threshing-floor.

He goes on Sunday to the church,
And sits among his boys;
He hears the parson pray and preach,
He hears his daughter's voice,
Singing in the village choir,
And it makes his heart rejoice.

It sounds to him like her mother's voice,
Singing in Paradise!
He needs must think of her once more,
How in the grave she lies;
And with his hard rough hand he wipes
A tear from out his eyes.

Toiling—rejoicing—sorrowing—
Onward through life he goes:
Each morning sees some task begin,
Each evening sees it close;
Something attempted—something done,
Has earned a night's repose.

Thanks, thanks to thee, my worthy friend,
For the lesson thou hast taught!
Thus at the flaming forge of Life,
Our fortunes must be wrought,
Thus on its sounding anvil shaped
Each burning deed and thought.